Blanche and Smitty

by Michele Malkin

BANTAM BOOKS

TORONTO · NEW YORK · LONDON · SYDNEY · AUCKLAND

BLANCHE AND SMITTY

A Bantam Book / July 1987

ISBN 0-553-05424-4

Published simultaneously in the United States and Canada

Bantam Books are published by Bantam Books, Inc.
Its trademark, consisting of the words "Bantam Books"
and the portrayal of a rooster, is Registered in U.S.
Patent and Trademark Office and in other countries.
Marca Registrada. Bantam Books, Inc., 666 Fifth Avenue,
New York, New York 10103.

PRINTED IN WEST GERMANY

0   9   8   7   6   5   4   3   2   1

To my mother and father

And to John, for all his encouragement

Once upon a time there was a girl named Blanche.

Blanche lived alone, in a house surrounded by green hills. She loved to read stories and paint pictures, especially landscapes.

In the spring and summer Blanche worked in her garden, where she grew lots of flowers and fresh vegetables.

Blanche often wore something red, because red was her favorite color.

One Christmas, Santa sent
Blanche a surprise. . . .

1

2

3

4

Blanche did not care for this present at all!

"I hope this cat was delivered to the wrong house," she said.

Blanche searched through the box for a tag that might have the right address. But, there was no such tag.

However, Blanche did find something else. . . .

"Not many cats come with a personalized bowling shirt," she thought. "This Smitty must be someone special.

"I really should give him a chance."

Blanche was not prepared for the demands of living with such a special cat.

She was alarmed by Smitty's enormous appetite.

Blanche was afraid that if she fed Smitty as much as he wanted, he would no longer fit in her living room.

1

2

3

4

In no time at all, Smitty had taken over the house.

Blanche thought it would be warm and cozy having Smitty around.

But, she learned that life doesn't always go smoothly when you have to share things.

1

2

3

4

Blanche was having trouble adjusting to Smitty's unpredictable behavior.

"I don't know what to do with him," said Blanche.

"Smitty is really beginning to get on my nerves."

Smitty brought out a crabby side to Blanche's personality she didn't know she had.

"He thinks he can do whatever he wants," said Blanche.

"Well, I'm the boss in this house!"

1

2

3

4

5

6

Blanche finally had had enough! She called Smitty over.

"I don't know what to do with you," said Blanche.

"I never asked for a cat. I wanted ice skates.

"Are you listening to me? I haven't had a moment's peace since you entered this house. You have been nothing but trouble!"

That night after dinner, the oddest thing happened.

Without even being asked, Smitty cleared the table and insisted on doing all the dishes.

Blanche had to pinch herself.

"This is just a dream. Any moment I'll wake up. . . ."

Smitty made an extraordinary effort to be nice.

Every morning he brought Blanche the newspaper, a plate of cinnamon toast, and a large chocolate milk.

Every afternoon he made her a bowl of soup and an assortment of sandwiches.

Blanche was impressed by the new Smitty.

"I've misjudged him," said Blanche. "I didn't realize how clever and charming he could be."

1

2

3

4

Smitty was thoughtful and considerate.

He cleaned the house, he ran errands, and he returned all the things that had mysteriously disappeared since his arrival.

"This is the real Smitty," said Blanche. "I knew all along he was a sweetheart."

But, Smitty could not keep up the charade forever. He started to crack under the constant strain of being sweet and undemanding.

One day, while preparing his famous submarine sandwich for Blanche, Smitty suddenly felt weak.

"I'll just have a taste," he thought. "One little taste . . ."

Smitty lost control and ate the whole thing.

Blanche found him slumped over the table.

"I have to admit," said Blanche as she helped him to the couch, "Smitty is not that easy to live with.

"But, he does add a certain spice to my life."

And so, Blanche realized that her life with Smitty would not always go as smoothly as she had hoped.

Smitty was full of surprises and Blanche would have to try her best to keep up with him.

And, once in a while, she did. . . .

1

2

3

4

The End